Marcia Brown

THE BLUE JACKAL

CHARLES SCRIBNER'S SONS · NEW YORK

To J.A.L.

Copyright © 1977 Marcia Brown

Library of Congress Cataloging in Publication Data
Brown, Marcia.
   The blue jackal.
   SUMMARY: A timid jackal becomes king of the forest
by virtue of his extraordinary color.
   [1. Folklore—India. 2. Jackals—Fiction] I. Title.
PZ8.1.B816Bl   [398.2]   76-54845
ISBN 0-684-14905-2

This book published simultaneously in the
United States of America and in Canada
Copyright under the Berne Convention

1 3 5 7 9 11 13 15 17 19 RD/C 20 18 16 14 12 10 8 6 4 2

Printed in the United States of America

The Blue Jackal is adapted from *The Panchatantra*, translated
from the Sanskrit by Arthur W. Ryder. Copyright 1956 by Mary
E. and Winfred Ryder. Used with permission of
The University of Chicago Press.

A jackal, called Fierce-Howl
for his fine voice,
lived in a cave in the barren hills
outside a city.

One night
his throat was so pinched with hunger
he ran into the city to see
what he could find to eat.

But the city dogs
snapped at his legs with their pointed teeth
and froze his heart
with their dreadful barking.

Fierce-Howl ran
and the dogs ran after him,
up one alley and down another,
until he stumbled into the open doorway
of a dyer's house.

With no thought
but to save his skin,
he jumped into a huge vat
of indigo.
The dogs gave up the chase
and went home.

Early in the morning
Fierce-Howl managed
to scramble out of the indigo vat
and escape to the forest.

But when the forest animals
caught sight of his beautiful blue fur,
they cried out, "Who is this,
blue like the sky?"

They fled,
their eyes popping with terror.

"Here is a creature
who has fallen from nowhere.
Who knows what he will do?"
The jackal saw their terror
and their awe.
He called to them,
"Come, you wild ones.
Why do you run from me?
The gods on high saw that
you forest folk had no king
and sent me to you.
Rest here, safe
between my peaceful paws."

When they heard this, the animals of the forest
bowed low and begged, "Master, how may we serve you?
Tell us our duties."

So the jackal appointed the lion Prime Minister and the tiger Lord of the Bedchamber. The leopard guarded the King's dish, the elephant watched the gate, and the monkey bore the royal parasol.

But his brother jackals Fierce-Howl cuffed and drove away.

So Fierce-Howl lived in glory.
The lion brought down the King's game,
and the leopard served the King's meat.
Fierce-Howl divided the meat and shared it
with a king's bounty.

One sleepy afternoon
Fierce-Howl's ears pricked up
and sent his crown rolling from his head.
A pack of jackals was howling on the hills.
Fierce-Howl's eyes filled with tears of joy.

His sleek fur stood on end.

He leaped up and lifted his muzzle and HOWLED.

When the lion and other animals heard him

they saw him for what he was and hung their heads.

"Our blue king is nothing but a jackal!
After him!"
And they chased the jackal
back to the cave in the barren hills.

"What is my place? My time? My friends?
Expenditure or dividends?
And what am I? And what my power?
So one must ponder hour by hour."